Chavela and the Magic Bubble

by **Monica Brown**

illustrated by **Magaly Morales**

CLARION BOOKS ⬦ Houghton Mifflin Harcourt ⬦ Boston • New York ⬦ 2010

The word chicle *(pronounced* chic-lay*) is the Spanish word for chewing gum. In English* chicle *(pronounced* chic-lay *or* chickle, *as in* pickle*) refers to the sap used as a base in natural chewing gums. In this story, it appears in* **script** *when it is in Spanish and in plain type when it refers to the gum base.*

To my very own Chavela, who inspired this book with her many magical questions —M.B.

To my sisters, Yuji and Elizabeth, my pride and inspiration —M.M.

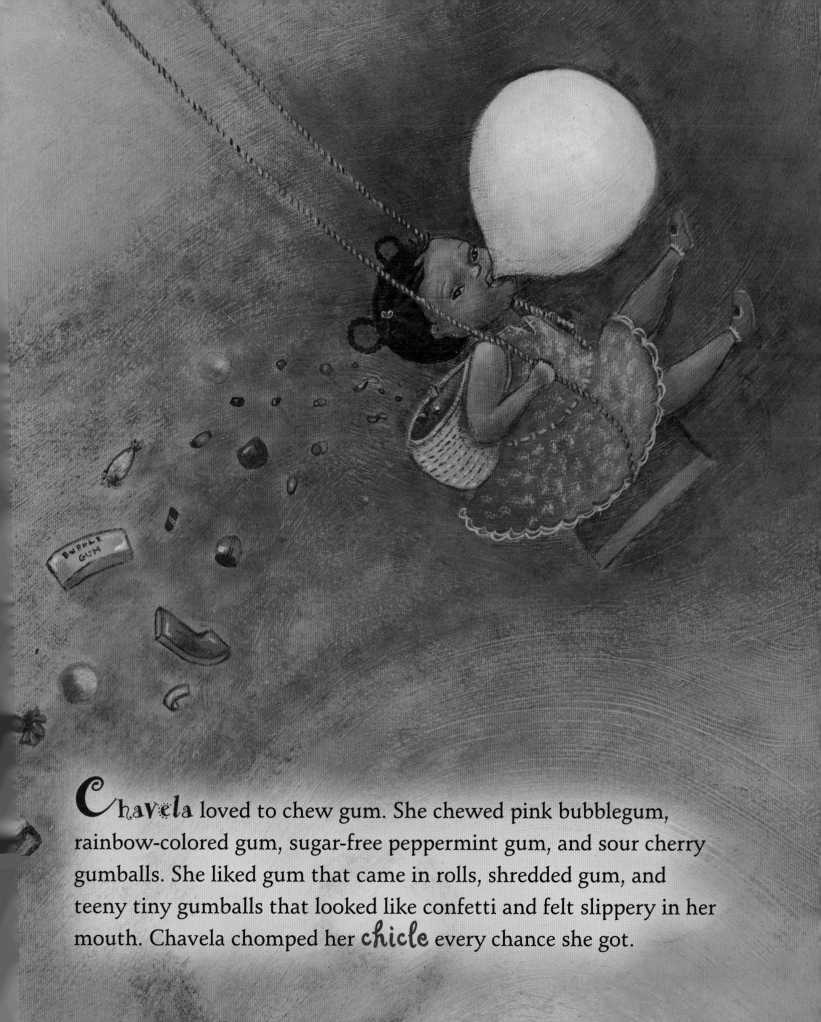

Chavela loved to chew gum. She chewed pink bubblegum,
rainbow-colored gum, sugar-free peppermint gum, and sour cherry
gumballs. She liked gum that came in rolls, shredded gum, and
teeny tiny gumballs that looked like confetti and felt slippery in her
mouth. Chavela chomped her chicle every chance she got.

Chavela was especially good at blowing bubbles.
She blew big bubbles shaped like pink balloons
and little bubbles the size of jellybeans.

She could blow **bubbles** inside of **bubbles** and two **bubbles** side by side, and one time she even blew a bubble shaped like a d**o**g.

On Saturdays, Chavela and her grandmother would split a piece of gum and go shopping on Market Street. Chavela's *abuelita* would tell her stories about the quiet town of Playa del Carmen, Mexico, where she grew up.

One morning Abuelita was telling Chavela about the beautiful rainforest and the birds and the butterflies that lived there, when Chavela blew a big bubble shaped like a butterfly! "Bravo!" said Abuelita.

IN THE RAINFOREST OF MEXICO THERE IS A MAGICAL

MAGIC CHICLE

SAPODILLA TREE, FROM THIS TREE OUR AMAZING CHICLE COMES

Chavela popped her bubble, and they went into a tiny corner store. Chavela spotted a kind of gum she had never seen before. Magic Chicle, the package read, in letters as blue as the sky. On the back it said, *"Deep in the rainforest of Mexico there is a magical sapodilla tree. From this tree our amazing chicle comes."* Chavela snatched it up and paid for it with a pocketful of coins.

On the way home, Chavela asked, "What does a tree have to do with gum?" "Well, Chavela," explained Abuelita, "gum is made from chicle, the sap of the sapodilla tree. Did you know that my father was a chiclero? Chicleros are workers who care for the sapodilla trees and harvest chicle from them."

"But why is the chicle magic?"

"That you will have to find out for yourself,"
Abuelita said with a smile.

Once home, Chavela ran straight to her room and opened her **Magic Chicle**. It smelled wildly delicious. She popped a piece in her mouth . . . and then another . . . and another. Yum! Soon the whole package was gone.

Chavela chewed and chewed and then took a deep breath and blew a great big bubble that got bigger ... and bigger ... and bigger ... and bigger until ...

Chavela's feet lifted off the ground and she *floated up* and out her bedroom window.

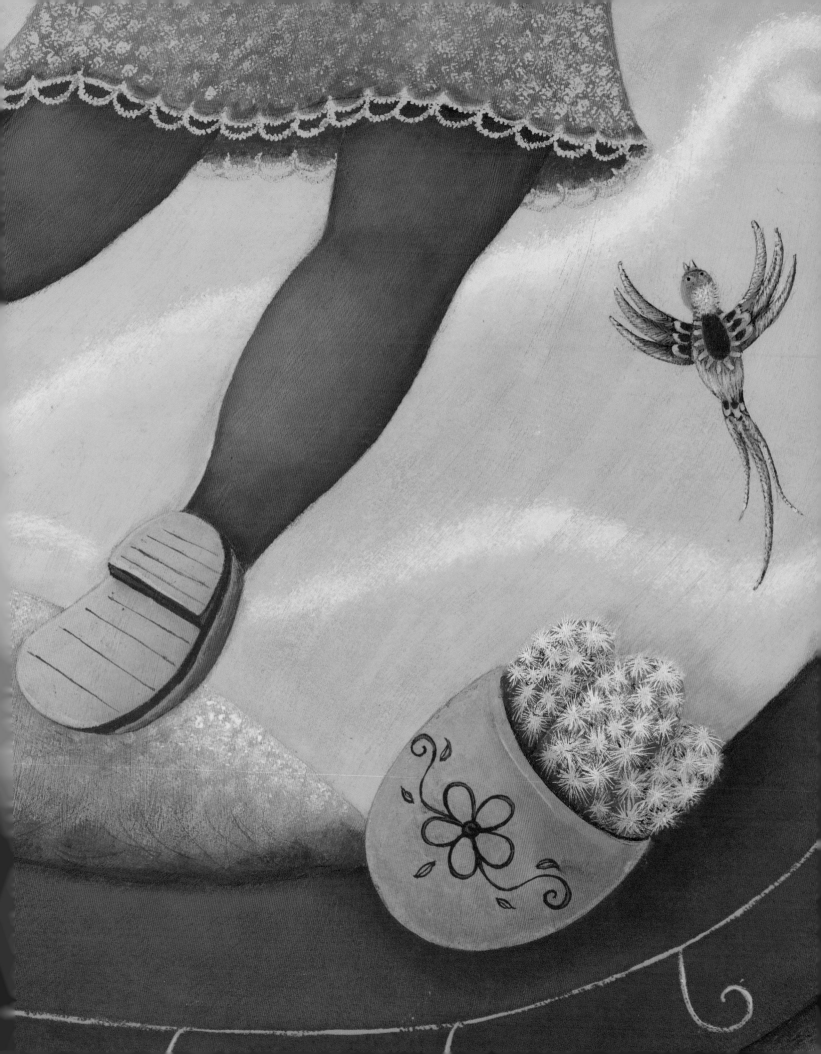

The wind swooped her over the mountains of California, across the deserts of Arizona, and past the rivers of Texas. Then the wind blew Chavela and her magic **bubble** south toward Mexico and the white sand beaches of Playa del Carmen. She smiled at the children playing by the water and spread her arms like a bird.

Chavela floated above the jungles of the Yucatán, bouncing along the tops of the lovely sapodilla trees.

Down below, *chicleros* were making zigzag cuts in the tree trunks and collecting the dripping chicle in big sacks. Children skipped around the trees, singing and holding hands. One little girl had a doll with a pretty blue dress. The girl waved and Chavela waved back.

Chavela floated softly down, landing under the tallest sapodilla tree of all. The little girl with the doll came right up to Chavela and said, "Hola! Do you like our magic tree?"

"Magic tree?" Chavela asked, her hand on the strong trunk. "Why is it magic?"

"Because it brings us visitors like you!" the little girl said with a wink. "Chicleros like my father collect chicle from these trees and send it to the United States to be made into chewing gum. But the chicle from this tree is special."

"My great-grandfather was a chiclero, and he cared for these trees too," said Chavela.

"I know," the little girl said mysteriously, handing Chavela the doll with the pretty blue dress. "Come and sing with us!"

Chavela held hands with the other children and together
they sang a song about the doll.

Tengo una muñeca vestida de azul . . .

I have a doll dressed up in blue . . .

Then they ran and played under the shade of the sapodilla
trees until Chavela became very tired. She wrapped herself up
in a pile of leaves and leaned against the magic tree. She watched
the butterflies and listened to the birds and the singing of the
chicleros, and soon she was fast asleep.

When Chavela woke up, the sun had set and the birds and the butterflies and the **chicleros** were gone. So were the little girl and the doll with the pretty blue dress. Chavela brushed the leaves away and shivered. She missed her **abuelita**. But she had already chewed all her magic gum. How would she ever get home?

Suddenly, she felt a drip on the tip of her nose. It was **soft** and **sticky**. It was chicle from the **magic** sapodilla tree!

Chavela popped the chicle into her mouth and chewed and chewed and blew and blew until . . . she floated **up** and **away** into the twinkling sky, back over mountains and deserts and cities, finally drifting down,

down,

down,

toward her little red house.

Plop! Chavela floated through the window and landed on her bed, happy and bouncy and full of magic. She ran to the kitchen to see her grandmother. "Long journey?" Abuelita asked with a wink.

"How did you know?" Chavela asked.

"I know because when I was a little girl, magic was part of my life too. And now I have a special present I've been waiting to give you," Abuelita said. Then she reached deep into her pocket and pulled out the doll with the pretty blue dress. "This was mine when I was a little girl, and now it's yours, just like the magic of the sapodilla tree."

Although Chavela was never again able to find **Magic Chicle** in the corner store, from then on, whenever she chewed her **chicle** she thought of her great-grandfather the **chiclero** and the little girl who grew up to be her grandmother—and the rainforest and the birds and the butterflies and the beauty of the whole wide world—and her **chicle** tasted even sweeter.

Author's Note

Rainforests such as the Gran Petén in southern Mexico and Central America are home to the tropical evergreen sapodilla tree. These beautiful trees are known for their sweet fruit, but they also produce a sticky sap, called chicle, that is used as a base in natural chewing gums.

Though chicle harvesting declined in the mid-1900s after most manufacturers started using synthetic substances to make gum, there are still workers called *chicleros* living in the Gran Petén, harvesting chicle and acting as stewards of the amazing sapodillas. The process for tapping the trees for chicle remains much the same as it has for hundreds of years. *Chicleros* climb high in the trees and make zigzag cuts in the trunks with machetes. The chicle drips from the cuts into containers set at the bottom of the trees. The *chicleros* then cook the chicle until it reaches the proper thickness and, once it has cooled, package it and send it to chewing gum manufacturers, where it is mixed with sugar and flavorings to make gum.

Rainforests are the most diverse and important ecosystems on our planet, but they are being destroyed at an astounding rate. In writing this book, it is my hope that readers will be enchanted by the beauty of the rainforests and the magical history of the sapodilla tree—and learn that they too can be stewards of nature, by recycling, conserving, and supporting environmentally friendly companies.

☆ To learn more about the harvesting process and the importance of sustainable farming practices, visit www.gleegum.com, the website of one of the few U.S. manufacturers of natural chewing gum.

☆ To learn more about rainforests and what you can do to help save them, visit www.rainforestfoundation.org and www.savetherainforest.org.

The song Chavela sings when she visits Mexico is called "Tengo una muñeca," or "I Have a Doll." All over Mexico and Latin America, mothers and grandmothers sing this song to their children and grandchildren. The song has many wonderful versions; this one is closest to the one my mother learned growing up in northern Peru.

TENGO UNA MUÑECA
I Have a Doll

Allegretto

Latin American folk song adapted by Monica Brown

1. Tengo u - na mu - ñe - ca ves - tida de a - zul,
2. La lle - vé a la pla - za se me res - fri - ó,
3. Dos y dos son cua - tro y dos son seis.
4. Brin - ca - mos la tab - li - ta, que ya la brin - qué

za - pa - ti - tos blan - cos y me - dias de tul.
la lle - vé al mé - di - co y le cu - ró.
Seis y seis son do - ce y cua - tro die - ci - séis.
brin - ca - mos la ot - ra vez que ya me can - sé.

1. I have a doll dressed up in blue
   with small white shoes and organza socks.

2. I took her to the plaza and she caught a cold.
   I took her to the doctor and he cured her.

3. Two and two is four and two is six.
   Six and six is twelve plus four is sixteen.

4. Let's jump the board; I already jumped!
   Let's jump again; I am much too tired.

Clarion Books ◇ 215 Park Avenue South, New York, New York 10003 ◇ Text copyright © 2010 by Monica Brown ◇ Illustrations copyright © 2010 by Magaly Morales ◇ The illustrations were executed in acrylics. ◇ The text was set in 16.5-point Schneidler BT. ◇ All rights reserved. ◇ For information about permission to reproduce selections from this book, write to Permissions, Houghton Mifflin Harcourt Publishing Company, 215 Park Avenue South, New York, New York 10003. ◇ Clarion Books is an imprint of Houghton Mifflin Harcourt Publishing Company. ◇ www.hmhbooks.com ◇ Manufactured in China ◇ Library of Congress Cataloging-in-Publication Data ◇ Brown, Monica, 1969– ◇ Chavela and the magic bubble / Monica Brown ; illustrated by Magaly Morales. ◇ p. cm. ◇ Summary: When Chavela blows a bubble with a strange new gum, she floats away to Mexico, where her great-grandfather once worked harvesting the tree sap that makes gum chewy. ◇ ISBN 978-0-547-24197-5 ◇ 1. Chewing gum—Fiction. 2. Magic—Fiction. 3. Grandmothers—Fiction. 4. Mexican Americans—Fiction.] I. Morales, Magaly, ill. II. Title. ◇ PZ7.B816644Ch 2010 ◇ [E]—dc22 ◇ 2009015819 ◇ LEO 10 9 8 7 6 5 4 3 2 1